FADE

FADE ROUTE

BUTTONHOOK

POST PATTERN

From left: Eli, Peyton, and Archie Manning.

The Mannings are the most famous family in football.

Peyton and Eli Manning are both star quarterbacks. They have led their teams to victory in the Super Bowl and won MVP trophies. Their older brother, Cooper, was an all-state wide receiver in high school and received a football scholarship to the University of Mississippi ("Ole Miss"). And their father, Archie, was a star quarterback for the New Orleans Saints.

Football has always been a big deal in the Manning family. Here is *Family Huddle*, written by Peyton, Eli, and Archie Manning. The picture book is based on some of the Mannings' family and football memories from their days in Louisiana and Mississippi.

FAMILY HUDDLE

Written by
PEYTON MANNING,
ELI MANNING,
and ARCHIE MANNING

Illustrations by
JIM MADSEN

Scholastic Press
New York

ISBN-13: 978-0-545-21351-6   ISBN-10: 0-545-21351-7

10 9 8 7 6 5 4 3 2 1   09 10 11 12 13

Reinforced Binding for Library Use

Printed in Mexico   49

First Club edition, September 2009

The display type was set in Acropolis. · The text was set in Times Roman.

The art was created using digital media.

Back cover and interior photo credit: Bill Frakes/Getty Images

Book design by Elizabeth B. Parisi

To Gan, PaPa, Sis, and Buddy.

rchie was in the front yard in New Orleans, playing with his three sons: Cooper, Peyton, and Eli. It was Peyton's turn at their favorite game, *Amazing Catches*.

"GO DEEP!" called Archie. It was the boys' favorite play.

Peyton ran full speed across the lawn. His dad threw the ball high and far. Peyton dived and caught the ball on his fingertips. He rolled to a stop in the grass as his brothers cheered. The neighbor's dog licked his face.

Olivia, their mom, was laughing on the front porch. "Nice catch, Peyton. You boys come in and wash up before we go! This weekend is going to be filled with family and football."

"All right, boys, let's wrap it up," said Dad.

"Come on, just one more play," shouted Eli. "I'll be the quarterback.
FADE ROUTE."

Once the car was packed, the boys stood together by the driveway. The football was hidden under Peyton's arm. As their mom and dad headed toward the car, Peyton handed the ball to Eli. Peyton and Cooper ran toward their parents, distracting them.

Eli ran the ball into the backseat of the car. It was a perfect

QUARTERBACK SNEAK. . . .

It was a l-o-n-g drive to Drew, Mississippi, where Archie's mom lived. The boys liked playing sports trivia games to pass the time. This one was called the *Numbers Game*.

"Thirty-four," said Cooper, sitting in the backseat with his brothers.

Peyton thought about it and came up with a football player who wore jersey number 34. "Walter Payton!" he said.

Next it was Peyton's turn: "Eight."

Before Cooper could answer, Eli called out, "My age and Dad's number!"

Cooper and Eli laughed out loud. They played the *Numbers Game* over and over again.

Archie stopped a block from his mom's small brick house and let the boys run the rest of the way. "Grandma Sis," they called. Their grandma heard them coming. She put down her knitting needles and picked up a plate of freshly baked chocolate chip cookies. She stepped outside and could see them zigzagging as they threw the football to each other.

"Hi, boys!" said Grandma Sis. "There's plenty of cookies for everyone!"

After lunch, everyone went outside for a group photograph. Olivia hugged the boys and said, "As long as you look out for each other, you will always be on a winning team." The boys giggled and then Eli hollered to Cooper and Peyton, "BUTTONHOOK." Then he took off across the yard.

Peyton smiled as Cooper snapped the ball back to him. He knew this play. "Get open, Eli!" he shouted.

It looked like Eli would run clear into the next lawn. Suddenly, he planted his foot and turned in toward his brothers. "Hit me, Peyt!" he said.

Peyton fired the pass. It was a perfect pass and a perfect catch, but Eli's foot landed in a puddle. Cooper and Peyton cracked up as Eli did a muddy dance.

Later that afternoon, they joined a football game near the town's fire station.

It was Peyton's turn at quarterback. Peyton handed the ball off to a teammate for a runaround, but the play did not work. The team lost yards.

Peyton looked over at the old fire truck and remembered his mother's words. Then he looked at Cooper and Eli.

"Eli, this one is for you,"
Peyton said. "Ring the alarm!"

They ran the HOOK AND LADDER play. Cooper was the best receiver, so he got the tricky part. Once the ball was snapped, he ran down the side of the field. Peyton hit him with a short pass. Cooper saw the defense coming his way. No one noticed little Eli running up behind him. Just as Cooper was being tackled, he flipped the ball back to Eli. "Go, E!" he shouted.

Eli caught the ball and ran for the touchdown!

Soon the boys were in the front yard. Eli was already on the bike he liked to ride around town. His brothers were getting ready to follow him when the postman came by with the mail. Eli pointed to the postman and hollered to them, "Are you thinking what I'm thinking?"

Cooper and Peyton didn't need to say a word. They'd come up with their own hand signals for some football plays. This was one of them: the POST PATTERN!

Peyton pressed his fingers together and made a slashing motion with his hand. He motioned at an angle toward the far side of the yard.

Cooper took off, using all his speed. He ran straight at first. Just as Peyton released a rainbow pass, Cooper cut in at an angle toward the center of the field. He stretched out his hands and caught the ball.

Eli watched everything from his bike. He laughed when he heard
Cooper call out, "The postman always delivers!"

When they returned to their grandparents' house, their mom was waiting on the porch. "Hurry and get ready; we have a long drive ahead of us."

They said good-bye to Gan Gan and PaPa. "We'll be back soon!" they said, waving their hands.

Eli, Peyton, and Cooper piled into the backseat.

"Thirteen," said Eli.

"That's easy—Dan Marino," said Peyton. The *Numbers Game* started again.

It was just getting dark when they got home. Their dad got out of the driver's seat. "I've got an idea," he said. "Why don't we finish that game?"

"Not too long," said Mom. "It's almost suppertime."

The boys looked over. Somehow their dad had gotten his hands on the football.

"Family huddle," Archie called. Eli, Peyton, and Cooper ran over to him and linked arms together and listened to the play. "Break, on one," their dad said, and they did. The brothers smiled and sprinted across the yard. Their mom was right—they were on a winning team!

QUARTERBACK SNEAK

GO DEEP

HOOK AND LADDER